D1327381

DESMOND COLE
GHOST PATROL

THE SHOW MUST DEMON!

by Andres Miedoso
illustrated by Victor Rivas

LITTLE SIMON
New York   London   Toronto   Sydney   New Delhi

LITTLE SIMON
An imprint of
Simon & Schuster Children's Publishing Division
1230 Avenue of the Americas, New York, New York 10020
First Little Simon hardcover edition April 2023
Copyright © 2023 by Simon & Schuster, Inc.
Also available in a Little Simon paperback edition.
All rights reserved, including the right of reproduction
in whole or in part in any form.
LITTLE SIMON is a registered trademark of Simon & Schuster, Inc.,
and associated colophon is a trademark of Simon & Schuster, Inc.
For information about special discounts for bulk purchases, please contact
Simon & Schuster Special Sales at 1-866-506-1949 or
business@simonandschuster.com.
The Simon & Schuster Speakers Bureau can bring authors to your
live event. For more information or to book an event contact the
Simon & Schuster Speakers Bureau at 1-866-248-3049
or visit our website at www.simonspeakers.com.
Designed by Steve Scott
Manufactured in the United States of America 0223 LAK
2 4 6 8 10 9 7 5 3 1
This book has been cataloged with the Library of Congress.
ISBN 978-1-6659-3379-7 (paperback)
ISBN 978-1-6659-3380-3 (hardcover)
ISBN 978-1-6659-3381-0 (ebook)

CONTENTS

CHAPTER ONE

STAGE FRIGHT

BOOK REPORT

Okay, before I even start this story, we need to talk about that icky feeling called "stage fright." Every kid ever has had stage fright before, right?

Maybe you needed to stand up in front of the class and give a report?

1

Maybe the teacher asked you to go up to the board and solve a math problem that you didn't know how to solve?

Maybe you were picked to read the school announcements over the intercom from the principal's office while the principal watches you to make sure you read everything just as it was written and . . . phew. I'm getting nervous just thinking about that!

Or maybe, just maybe, you have found yourself on an actual stage in front of an actual audience filled with every kid from school . . . AND THEIR PARENTS . . . while you try to remember your lines.

That's when you get the feeling you have right now, just thinking about all this, picturing yourself in those situations.

Your stomach is doing flips. You have no idea what to do with your hands all of a sudden. Like, what are your hands even for?

And your mouth is so dry that you think a desert moved in there. And your mind just went as blank as the eyes that are staring back at you, just waiting for you to do something . . . anything.

Well, that, my friend, is *stage fright*, and it is *the worst*!

But I have good news.

There are ways to get over stage fright! First, remember that everyone gets stage fright sometimes, so you're not alone.

Except for on that stage, with the audience staring at you . . . Hmm, I guess you are totally alone. Okay, forget about that first bit of advice and focus on this one.

Because I have a story that should help you totally get over stage fright.

See, I used to be scared of everything until I met my best friend, Desmond Cole. He'd convinced me to enter the variety show at school,

which was not easy because of how much I didn't want to go on that stage.

But then he said the words that both helped and haunted me forever: *How bad can it be?*

Well, let me show you how bad.

That's me, Andres Miedoso, sur-rounded by giant bunnies with giant teeth and giant fluffy tails that may sound really cute, but trust me, they weren't cute.

ANDRES MIEDOSO

And that's Desmond trapped in the box with the saw trying to cut him in half.

And the demon running around the stage while being chased by a pack of adorable puppies? Well, that's kind of a longer story.

DESMOND COLE

CHAPTER TWO

THE SIGN-UP SHEET

It started like a lot of stage fright stories start: with a sign-up sheet.

It was just sitting on the wall, looking totally normal and hung up with thumbtacks next to the creepy posters drawn by all the kids in the kindergarten class.

Teachers and parents thought pictures drawn by little kids were cute. But if you asked me, they were *scary*!

Stick figures with long legs and big heads with bigger mouths? Families who looked like zombies holding flowers? Puppy dogs the size of skyscrapers? And is that supposed to be a horse or an alien creature?

"It's totally an alien creature," Desmond said, as if he were reading my mind.

"How can you tell?" I asked. "Wait, have you seen aliens before?"

But Desmond doesn't always answer questions, and today was one of those days. He just smiled at me, like he probably had seen an alien before, then pointed at the sign-up sheet.

"Are you here to sign up for the variety show?" Desmond asked.

He grabbed the pencil that was dangling from a string and added his name to the list.

"Variety show?" I asked. "What's that?"

"We do it every year," Desmond said. "It's really fun. Kids sign up to perform anything they want onstage in front of an audience."

"What do you mean the kids perform?" I asked.

"Oh, like, every kid has a special talent, and they get to perform that talent onstage and everyone claps and cheers for them," Desmond explained.

"Special talents . . . like superheroes?" I let out a gasp. "Do we
go to school with any superheroes?
If we do, you have to tell me, that's
the best-friend code."

"What? No!" Desmond said. "At
least, I don't think so."

Then Desmond and I scanned the hallway, looking for anyone who might be a superhero in disguise. We didn't see anything out of the ordinary.

"Anyway," Desmond continued, "when I say 'talent,' I mean some kids sing a song, some kids dance, some kids juggle. One time there was a kid who scooped ice cream and then threw the scoops across the stage, where they each landed in a stack on top of a single ice cream cone! It was amazing!"

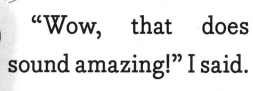

"Wow, that does sound amazing!" I said.

"I know!" Desmond said. "That's why I sign up every year!"

"So is your talent going to have anything to do with . . . the Ghost Patrol?" I whispered.

"Huh?" Desmond looked confused. "Oh, nah. I've got other tricks up my sleeve. You'll see. Especially when you sign up for the show too!"

Desmond picked up the pencil on a string again and handed it to me.

"No thanks," I said. "I don't really have a talent. Plus, I always get stage fright."

"Okay," said Desmond as he dropped the pencil. It swung back and forth on its string. "But when someone juggles piñatas full of candy

this year and lets the piñatas crack open and gives all the performers candy, don't come crying to me because you didn't sign up."

I shrugged because I wasn't sure what I was supposed to say to that.

Then we went to class.

But maybe I should have stayed a few more seconds, because then I would have seen the shadow watching us . . . and stopped that shadow from its very, very evil plan.

CHAPTER THREE

MR. TIMPANI

Music class is a weird thing for kids.

Not every kid plays music, but for some reason every kid is *forced* to learn how to play the recorder.

The recorder is a plastic instrument that's one step above a kazoo.

If you play it right, it kinda sounds okay. But if you are like me (and like most kids), you play it wrong, and it sounds like a cat is in a lot of trouble.

One time I was practicing at home, and I must have hit some really bad notes, because next thing I knew, my room was filled with stray cats. Hmm, maybe I should have closed the window.

"Good morning, class!" Mr. Timpani sang out.

Mr. Timpani is our music teacher. He's really nice. He's patient, kind, and always supportive of kids like me (who can't play music).

First, we ran through our scales, which is when the music notes go up and down in order.

Desmond was great at the recorder. His scales sounded like a real musician played them.

Mine sounded like mosquitos buzzing around your ears—high-pitched and super buggy.

After that, we practiced a song called "Baby Shark." You probably know it just by me saying the name. And I'll bet that song is stuck in your head right now!

Well, if you heard our class playing "Baby Shark," you'd forget it right away.

In fact, I bet we chased every shark away for miles because it sounded so bad. Hmm, remind me to bring the recorder the next time I go to the beach.

But even with all the loud, horrible notes, Mr. Timpani smiled and kept cheering us on.

He'd say things like "I love your gusto, Gary!" or "Yes, Desmond! I dig it!" or "Keep up the good work, Wanda!" or "Andres, I can't hear you—play louder."

Believe me, no one had ever asked me to play the recorder louder.

So I did. And guess what?

I still stank.

But I didn't care! Because Mr. Timpani made me feel like I could play the recorder in a sold-out orchestra event!

So, while I wasn't too fond of going to music class, Mr. Timpani made everything one hundred times better.

Still, that didn't prepare me for what came next. See, at the end of our class, Mr. Timpani made an announcement.

He was going to help out with the variety show this year, and he was thrilled to see so many kids had already signed up.

Then he held up the sign-up sheet
from outside and said, "Especially
you, Andres! I can't wait to see what
your talent will be!"

"Wait, what?" I asked.

"You signed up," Mr. Timpani said. "Right here!"

He pointed to the last name on the list. And it wasn't any old name. It was my name.

Gulp.

CHAPTER FOUR

RULES ARE RULES

Andres Miedoso

I raised my hand and said, "Mr. Timpani, I believe there's been some sort of mistake. I didn't sign up for anything."

"Of course you did, Andres," said Mr. Timpani. "Your name is right here."

He let me hold the sign-up sheet, and sure enough, my name was on there. But it wasn't my handwriting.

It was written in some very fancy cursive letters that I could hardly read it at first. But Desmond confirmed that it was my name.

"But that's not my handwriting!" I said. Then I showed how I write my name, which is only a little better than how I play the recorder.

After I was finished, I said, "See! I didn't sign up for anything!"

That's when Desmond tapped me on the shoulder. "Except you just did, Andres. You literally just wrote your name on the sign-up sheet."

Aw, crumbs, he was right.

"Rules are rules," Mr. Timpani said. "If you sign up on the sign-up sheet, you've got to perform!"

Well, I couldn't argue with that . . . especially because all the other students and my teacher *saw me write my name on the sheet!*

As we left music class, I had no idea what to do.

Desmond was sure it would be fine, but he never knew about all the other times my, um, *talents* had gone wrong.

One time I tried telling jokes, but somehow, I made the whole audience cry. And not in the good way.

One time I tried juggling, but some other kids had brought their dogs for their talents, and let me tell you, dogs love chasing balls. Even while you're trying to juggle.

And one time I tried just reading from a book. Sounds simple, right?

Well, apparently dogs like to chew on books too. Let's just say I don't have the best history with dogs and variety shows.

Then Desmond had an idea. "Hey, Andres, there's no rule that we can't work together. Why don't you join me as my assistant?"

"Maybe?" was all I could say. "What's your talent?"

"Magic!" Desmond whispered so no one else around could hear him.

"Wait," I said. "Does that mean I have to be the rabbit that gets pulled out of a hat?"

"Nah," said Desmond. "It's not that kind of magic."

"Do I have to get into a cauldron full of steamy gross things, like eye of newt?" I asked.

You had to think of every possible weird thing ever when you deal with Desmond Cole.

"Nah," said Desmond. "It's not *that* kind of magic either. It's just a simple magic act. I'll show you everything after school."

Okay. Suddenly, I wasn't worried about my stage fright. Nope. Not at all.

Now I was only scared of what Desmond's magic act was going to be.

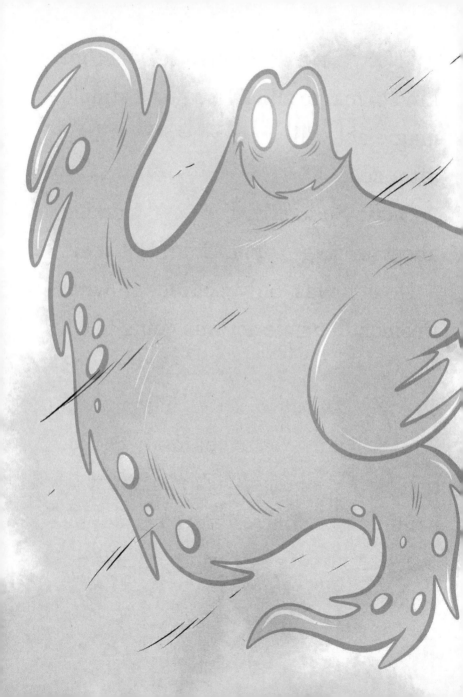

CHAPTER FIVE

NOT-SO-MAGIC ZAX

The last person I expected to see at Desmond's house after school was Zax, the ghost who lives at my house.

I guess technically Zax is a ghost, not a person, but what surprised me was that he was over at another kid's place!

"Are you ready to practice, Desmond?" Zax asked as he swooped over to us with a big smile on his ghost face. "I've been working on your trick all day."

"Oh," Desmond said nervously as he looked over at me. "Um, about the assistant position . . . Andres is going to take over for you."

"What?!" snapped Zax.

His eyes started to glow red before they chilled out.

"I mean, um, yeah, that's totally cool," he said. "I didn't really want to be in a school play or whatever. I was just trying to help. You know ghosts love to help."

"I'm sorry, Zax," I said. "It's just that someone signed me up for the variety show, and now I need to do something for it, and Desmond thought I could help him. So, you *are* kind of helping me out by letting me be Desmond's assistant?"

Zax thought about that, then he smiled. "By goodness, you are right! I *am* still helping out . . . and now I don't even have to worry about the sharp, rusty saw! Yay!"

Then that ghost flew through a wall and zoomed back to my house faster than I had ever seen him move.

"The sharp, rusty saw?" I asked. "What sharp, rusty saw?"

"Step this way, Andres!" said Desmond. "All will be discovered as soon as we go to my magic workshop."

By magic workshop, Desmond meant his garage. Most people keep cars in their garages, but not Desmond. Nope.

He had a box big enough to fit a kid like me inside it. The me-size box sat on a table with wheels, so it could be spun around.

"What's in the box, Desmond?" I asked with a gulp.

"Nothing, silly," said Desmond. Then he opened it and showed me it was empty. "At least nothing until you climb inside."

I didn't like the sound of that.

"Why do you need me in the box?"
I asked.

"So I can cut you in half," Desmond
said. "With this!"

Then Desmond pulled out the biggest saw I'd ever seen. Though, to be
fair, I don't think I'd ever seen a saw
in real life, so it was the *only* saw I'd
ever seen. But I still didn't like seeing those sharp, pointy teeth.

"You know, I'd hate to steal all the fun from Zax by being your assistant," I said. "Maybe we can let Zax go in the box, and I can be your cheering assistant. The one who sits far away from the box . . . in the audience . . . and claps for you after your trick is done."

"Um, my parents already have that job," said Desmond. "And Zax was so excited to help you out with your problem that I can't ask him to come back."

I looked around the garage and said, "That's true . . . but do you have any other tricks? Maybe one that doesn't cut anyone in half?"

"Sure!" said Desmond. "We could do the disappearing box, but I'd have to send you to another dimension."

"Pass," I said.

"Okay, that's fair," said Desmond. "There's the zigzag box, but it might hurt your spine."

"Pass," I said again.

"Gotcha," said Desmond. "Well, I could levitate you, but I don't know how to get the assistant back down yet. Zax just kept floating away. Oh, wait, I know. How long can you hold your breath under water?"

As Desmond continued naming tricks, the getting-sawed-in-half trick started to sound like the best one.

"Okay, okay, okay," I said. "I'll get in the box. But you've got to promise I'll be safe."

"Andres," Desmond said smoothly. "When have I ever put you in danger?"

CHAPTER SIX

OVER-THE-TOP

Magicians never reveal their secrets. The same goes for the assistants they saw in half.

So, I can't tell you about our magic practice.

But I can tell you that Desmond did keep me safe.

That didn't mean I didn't still have stage fright. I was not looking forward to performing in front of people at the variety show.

However, the one thing that I *was* looking forward to was working with Mr. Timpani.

I mean, he was really the nicest teacher at our school! If he could

make music class fun, our variety show practice was going to be great.

"Okay, everyone," Mr. Timpani cheered. "Let's get this rehearsal started. I'm ready to be dazzled!"

It was wild seeing all the other kids performing their talents. We had a very gifted class, apparently.

Dela Diva went first. She sang an original song that sounded like it should already be on the radio! She didn't have any sign of stage fright. Suddenly, I thought maybe this variety show would actually be fun.

But when Dela was done, Mr. Timpani jumped up, clapped super loud, and said, "That was fantastic! Truly fantastic! I have only one note. Right now you are trapped on the stage. A true performer would take up as much space as possible."

Then he looked up at the ceiling.

"Have you ever sang while flying through the air?" Mr. Timpani asked.

"No," said Dela. "I'm afraid of heights."

"Well, I am afraid of hosting a boring show," said Mr. Timpani.

"We've got to *wow* the audience. So, I'm going to install a trapeze for you. You will sing while flying over the crowd with no net!"

Then I saw it. The look on Dela's face said it all. It was going to be a stage fright night!

One by one, Mr. Timpani had the scariest ideas for each act. He wanted every performance to be as over-the-top and have as much flare and pizzaz as possible.

If a kid played the recorder, then Mr. Timpani wanted to have fireworks going off around them.

If a kid did the Hula-Hoop, Mr. Timpani wanted them to juggle swords at the same time.

If a kid did card tricks, Mr. Timpani wanted them to use giant cards so the audience could see everything.

There was even a dance group that did backflips and front flips and spun around on their heads. I didn't know what could be added to make it any wilder.

But Mr. Timpani did.

"I have one small suggestion," he said. "You should add puppies that dance! I'll get the puppies. All you need to do is teach them your moves!"

Welp. If I thought I was worried about stage fright before, I was super worried now.

But Desmond didn't even break a sweat.

When Mr. Timpani called our names, Desmond just stood up and said, "Mr. Timpani, we want to keep our trick a secret, but I promise it's a cut above the rest of the show."

Mr. Timpani smiled, and it wasn't the super-caring smile he usually gave students. It actually looked kind of evil.

"Excellent, Desmond and Andres," he snarled. "In that case you will be our closing act. And I hope you really bring down the house."

CHAPTER SEVEN

PRACTICE MAKES PERFECT

The weeks leading to the big show had everyone nervous and excited.

Well, mostly nervous. And scared.

All of Kersville was filled with the strangest things going wrong. And that's saying a lot for this weird little town.

We had already seen vampires, ghosts, mummies, and more.

I mean, we'd even seen a Surfin' Bird ride a drone!

But as soon as you thought you'd seen it all, Kersville was ready to surprise you again. Only this time things weren't haunted.

It started when the kids were practicing their new variety show acts. Dela Diva stopped taking singing lessons and signed up for trapeze lessons. The only problem was that she couldn't bring herself to climb the ladder.

And when she did . . . the Kersville fire department had to get her back down.

Actually, the Kersville Fire Department stayed pretty busy during those few weeks.

The recorder player's parents set off fireworks while she played.
It wasn't the brightest idea.

The card trick kid tried a new deck of giant cards. But the cards were so big that they kept blowing away and getting caught in the trees.

Plus, the Hula-Hoop kid tried to learn how to juggle, but decided to start small. So instead of using swords, she used her mom's good napkins.

Well, when her mom saw how dirty those good napkins got, she called in the fire department to clean them.

And the dance group with the puppies . . . Believe it or not, they actually taught those puppies how to dance! I swear, it was very impressive. They could really shake a tail.

Which brought me back to Desmond's magic workshop.

"Do you think our trick is tricky enough for Mr. Timpani?" I asked Desmond.

But it was Zax who flew in and answered, "Not tricky enough? What do you mean?"

So, we told Zax about the fireworks, the swords, the puppies, and
how Mr. Timpani kept trying to take
over everyone's acts to make them
way bigger and out of control.

"Oh," said Zax. "Sounds like your
teacher is a demon."

"I wouldn't say he's *that* bad,"
Desmond answered.

But Zax shook his ghost head. "No, I mean, he's really a demon. Demons love to take over people's lives. They also love putting on a show in front of an audience. But more than anything, demons love to frighten kids."

"And what better way to do that than to give kids the ultimate stage fright!" I gasped.

Suddenly, I knew Zax was right. Mr. Timpani, my favorite teacher in the whole school, was a demon. And he had to be dealt with . . . by the Ghost Patrol.

CHAPTER EIGHT

BACKSTAGE BEASTS

There is never a good time to deal with a demon. Especially on the night of your school's variety show.

So what else could we do? We arrived with our special box on wheels and hoped for the best.

Mr. Timpani was very impressed.

"Oh, you didn't tell me this would be a magic trick! How exciting!"

"Yep," I said. "Desmond is going to cut me in half with this sharp, rusty saw."

Now, I can't quite describe the glimmer of joy in Mr. Timpani's eyes. It was a sort of happiness and excitement you might have if you won the lottery.

"I love it," the demon teacher said. "But you need one more thing."

Then he pulled out a top hat and put it on Desmond's head.

"There," he said. "Now you look like a real magician."

"Thanks, I guess," said Desmond.

"Okay, everyone!" Mr. Timpani cheered to the students backstage. "Your parents, your grandparents, your sisters, your brothers, your teachers, and your fellow students will be watching. So make sure you don't mess up. That would be *perfectly* terrible."

All the kids suddenly looked nervous. The dance group's knees were shaking like the puppies' tails next to them.

The card trick kid dropped his pack of giant cards.

Dela Diva was trapped high above the stage.

The only kid who didn't look worried was the Hula-Hoop girl. And that did *not* make Mr. Timpani happy.

"You look . . . excited," Mr. Timpani said. "Did you learn how to juggle yet?"

"I did!" she said. "But not swords, like you wanted. I'm using bowling pins, which is just as cool."

"Tsk-tsk-tsk," said Mr. Timpani. "Bowling pins are so boring. Why not try these?"

Then he pulled out a stack of creepy bones that made my skin crawl. But that's not all those bones did.

Because not everyone is afraid of creepy bones. In fact, you know who loves bones? Puppies.

And hungry puppies are hard to stop.

CHAPTER NINE

BREAK A LEG

~~GOOD LUCK~~

Did you know that if someone is performing onstage, you should never wish them good luck? Apparently, that brings them bad luck.

Instead, you're supposed to say, *Break a leg*. But that night, I think we broke just about *everything*!

As soon as Mr. Timpani pulled out those creepy bones, all the hungry puppies charged. They knocked over Desmond, who lost his fancy top hat and stumbled into the magic box.

Guess what jumped out of the top hat? Yep, giant bunnies with giant teeth.

Why? Because Mr. Timpani was trying to make our magic show over-the-top.

But now he was cornered by a pack of hungry puppies. And here's what you should never do: corner a demon.

Suddenly, Mr. Timpani changed into his true demon self.

He had horns on his head, wings

on his back, and he looked like a
pro-wrestler.

"GET BACK, YOU PUPPIES!" he
boomed.

But puppies don't listen to any-
body. Not even demons.

Then I looked at the clock, and it was almost showtime . . . but this wasn't the kind of show that parents and teachers probably wanted to see. If anyone was going to save the variety show, it was gonna have to be me.

"Stop!" I yelled, and believe it or not, everyone listened. "Mr. Timpani, I know you're a demon, but I also know you're the best teacher at this school. And I know you only want the best performance ever, which is why you keep pushing us to do wild versions of our acts. But you don't need to do that. This audience just wants to cheer for their kids. They don't need fireworks or dancing puppies or giant bunnies leaping out of magic hats. So, let's go out there and break a leg."

All the kids stared at me. The puppies did too.

"Oh yeah,—'break a leg' means 'good luck' in the theater," I said, because clearly the other kids didn't know that yet.

Mr. Timpani smiled like his old self again and tossed the bones to the puppies.

"You're right," he said. "I wanted to make the biggest show ever, but I forgot what the audience wants: awkward pictures of their weird human kids onstage. Oh . . . I love awkward kid pictures!"

"So . . . why can't we just do what we want to do?" I asked.

"Yes, of course," said Mr. Timpani. "Students, I'm sorry. And Andres, I'm glad I signed your name on the sign-up sheet."

"You did that?" asked Desmond. "Why?"

"Because sometimes talented students just need a little nudge," said Mr. Timpani. And maybe that's why he was my favorite teacher.

CHAPTER TEN

THE SHOW MUST DEMON!

If you want to know how the variety show went, it was . . . meh.

Dela Diva forgot the words to her song and ended up humming "Baby Shark" instead. (Yeah, she couldn't even remember the words to "Baby Shark"!)

The Hula-Hoop girl accidentally threw her hoop into the audience and had to ask for it back.

And the dance group ... Well, they were doing pretty good ... until the puppies had to go to the bathroom. Then it got a little, um, slippery.

But none of that mattered to the audience. The parents and teachers cheered and clapped and whistled for every kid. In fact, each act got a standing ovation—even mine and Desmond's!

Plus, the applause thrilled Mr. Timpani more than stage fright!

I guess demons are weird that way.

So now Mr. Timpani hosts all the school plays. But don't worry. He only goes over-the-top every now and again.